Israel Zangwill

Chosen Peoples

Outlook

Israel Zangwill

Chosen Peoples

1. Auflage | ISBN: 978-3-73261-712-8

Erscheinungsort: Paderborn, Deutschland

Erscheinungsjahr: 2018

Outlook Verlag GmbH, Paderborn.

Reproduction of the original.

Israel Zangwill

Chosen Peoples

Outlook

WORKS
OF
ISRAEL ZANGWILL

CHOSEN PEOPLES

THE AMERICAN JEWISH BOOK COMPANY
NEW YORK
1921

─────────────

Printed by
The Lord Baltimore Press
Baltimore, Md.

─────────────

CHOSEN PEOPLES

Being The First "Arthur Davis Memorial Lecture"
delivered before the Jewish Historical Society
at University College on Easter-Passover
Sunday, 1918/5678

———————

TO

MRS. REDCLIFFE N. SALAMAN

THIS LITTLE BOOK IN HER
FATHER'S MEMORY

———————

CONTENTS

NOTE

The Arthur Davis Memorial Lecture was founded in 1917, under the auspices of the Jewish Historical Society of England, by his collaborators in the translation of "The Service of the Synagogue," with the object of fostering Hebraic thought and learning in honour of an unworldly scholar. The Lecture is to be given annually in the anniversary week of his death, and the lectureship is to be open to men or women of any race or creed, who are to have absolute liberty in the treatment of their subject.

FOREWORD

Mr. Arthur Davis, in whose memory has been founded the series of Lectures devoted to the fostering of Hebraic thought and learning, of which this is the first, was born in 1846 and died on the first day of Passover, 1906. His childhood was spent in the town of Derby, where there was then no Synagogue or Jewish minister or teacher of Hebrew. Spontaneously he developed a strong Jewish consciousness, and an enthusiasm for the Hebrew language, which led him to become one of its greatest scholars in this, or any other, country.

He was able to put his learning to good use. He observed the wise maxim of Leonardo da Vinci, "Avoid studies of which the result dies with the worker." He was not one of those learned men, of whom there are many examples—a recent and conspicuous instance was the late Lord Acton— whose minds are so choked with the accumulations of the knowledge they have absorbed that they can produce little or nothing. His output, though not prolific, was substantial. In middle life he wrote a volume on "The Hebrew Accents of the Twenty-one Books of the Bible," which has become a classical authority on that somewhat recondite subject. It was he who originated and planned the new edition of the Festival Prayer Book in six volumes, and he wrote most of the prose translations. When he died, though only two volumes out of the six had been published, he left the whole of the text complete. To Mr. Herbert M. Adler, who had been his collaborator from the beginning, fell the finishing of the great editorial task.

Not least of his services lay in the fact that he had transmitted much of his knowledge to his two daughters, who have worthily continued his tradition of Hebrew scholarship and culture.

Arthur Davis's life work, then, was that of a student and interpreter of Hebrew. It is a profoundly interesting fact that, in our age, movements have been set on foot in more than one direction for the revival of languages which were dead or dying. We see before our eyes Welsh and Irish in process of being saved from extinction, with the hope perhaps of restoring their ancient glories in poetry and prose. Such movements show that our time is not so utilitarian and materialistic as is often supposed. A similar revivifying process is affecting Hebrew. For centuries it has been preserved as a ritual language, sheltered within the walls of the Synagogue; often not fully understood, and never spoken, by the members of the congregations. Now it is becoming in Palestine once more a living and spoken language.

Hebrew is one example among many of a language outliving for purposes of ritual its use in ordinary speech. A ritual is regarded as a sacred thing, unchanging, and usually unchangeable, except as the result of some great religious upheaval. The language in which it is framed continues fixed, amid the slowly developing conditions of the workaday world. Often, indeed, the use of an ancient language, which has gradually fallen into disuse among the people, is deliberately maintained for the air of mystery and of awe which is conveyed by its use, and which has something of the same effect upon the intellect as the "dim religious light" of a cathedral has upon the emotions. Further, it reserves to the priesthood a kind of esoteric knowledge, which gives them an additional authority that they would desire to maintain. So we find that in the days of Marcus Aurelius an ancient Salian liturgy was used in the Roman temples which had become almost unintelligible to the worshippers. The ritual of the religion of Isis in Greece was, at the same period, conducted in an unknown tongue. In the present age Church Slavonic, the ecclesiastical language of the orthodox Slavs, is only just intelligible to the peasantry of Russia and the neighbouring Slav countries. The Buddhists of China conduct their services in Sanscrit, which neither the monks nor the people understand, and the services of the Buddhists in Japan are either in Sanscrit or in ancient Chinese. I believe it is a fact that in Abyssinia, again, the liturgy is in a language called Geez, which is no longer in use as a living tongue and is not understood.

But we need not go to earlier centuries or to distant countries for examples. In any Roman Catholic church in London to-day you will find the service conducted in a language which, if understood at all by the general body of the congregation, has been learnt by them only for the purposes of the liturgy.

Of all these ritual languages which have outlived their current use and have been preserved for religious purposes alone, Hebrew is, so far as I am aware, the only one which has ever showed signs of renewing its old vitality—like the roses of Jericho which appear to be dead and shrivelled but which, when placed in water, recover their vitality and their bloom. We may join in hoping that again in Palestine Hebrew may recover something of its old supremacy in the field of morals and of intellect.

To render this possible the work of scholars such as Arthur Davis has contributed. To him this was a labour of love, and for love. He would receive no payment for any of his religious work or writings. Part of the profits that accrued from the publication of his edition of "The Services of the Synagogue" has been devoted to the formation of a fund from which will be defrayed the expenses—after the first—of a series of annual lectures on subjects of Jewish interest, to be delivered by men of various schools of thought. We are fortunate that the initial lecture is to be delivered to-day by the most distinguished of living Jewish men of letters.

Arthur Davis was a man of much elevation and charm of character. He took an active part in the work of communal, and particularly educational, organizations. He was one of those men—not rare among Jews, though the rest of the world does not always recognize it—who are philanthropic in spirit, practical in action, modest, self-sacrificing, devoted to a fine family life, having in them much of the student and something even of the saint. It is fitting that his memory should be kept alive.

HERBERT SAMUEL.

CHOSEN PEOPLES

CHOSEN PEOPLES

I

The claim that the Jews are a "Chosen People" has always irritated the Gentiles. "From olden times," wrote Philostratus in the third century, "the Jews have been opposed not only to Rome but to the rest of humanity." Even Julian the Apostate, who designed to rebuild their Temple, raged at the doctrine of their election. Sinai, said the Rabbis with a characteristic pun, has evoked *Sinah* (hatred).

In our own day, the distinguished ethical teacher, Dr. Stanton Coit, complains, like Houston Chamberlain, that our Bible has checked and blighted all other national inspiration: in his book "The Soul of America," he even calls upon me to repudiate unequivocally "the claim to spiritual supremacy over all the peoples of the world."

The recent revelation of racial arrogance in Germany has provided our enemies with a new weapon. "Germanism is Judaism," says a writer in the American *Bookman*. The proposition contains just that dash of truth which is more dangerous than falsehood undiluted; and the saying ascribed to Von Tirpitz in 1915 that the Kaiser spent all his time praying and studying Hebrew may serve to give it colour. "As he talks to-day at Potsdam and Berlin," says Verhaeren, in his book "Belgium's Agony," "the Kings of Israel and their prophets talked six thousand years ago at Jerusalem." The chronology is characteristic of anti-Semitic looseness: six thousand years ago the world by Hebrew reckoning had not been created, and at any rate the then Kings of Jerusalem were not Jewish. But it is undeniable that Germanism, like Judaism, has evolved a doctrine of special election. Spiritual in the teaching of Fichte and Treitschke, the doctrine became gross and narrow in the

Deutsche Religion of Friedrich Lange. "The German people is the elect of God and its enemies are the enemies of the Lord." And this German God, like the popular idea of Jehovah, is a "Man of War" who demands "eye for eye, tooth for tooth," and cries with savage sublimity:—

> I will render vengeance to Mine adversaries,
>
> And will recompense them that hate Me,
> I will make Mine arrows drunk with blood,
> And my sword shall devour flesh.

Judaism has even its Song of Hate, accompanied on the timbrel by Miriam. The treatment of the Amalekites and other Palestine tribes is a byword. "We utterly destroyed every city," Deuteronomy declares; "the men and the women and the little ones; we left none remaining; only the cattle we took for a prey unto ourselves with the spoil of the cities." David, who is promised of God that his seed shall be enthroned for ever, slew surrendered Moabites in cold blood, and Judas Maccabæus, the other warrior hero of the race, when the neutral city of Ephron refused his army passage, took the city, slew every male in it, and passed across its burning ruins and bleeding bodies. The prophet Isaiah pictures the wealth of nations—the phrase is his, not Adam Smith's—streaming to Zion by argosy and caravan. "For that nation and kingdom that will not serve thee shall perish…. Aliens shall build up thy walls, and their kings shall minister unto thee. Thou shalt suck the milk of nations." "The Lord said unto me," says the second Psalm, "Thou art My son, this day have I begotten thee. Ask of Me and I will give the nations for thine inheritance…. Thou shalt break them with a rod of iron."

Nor are such ideas discarded by the synagogue of to-day. Every Saturday night the orthodox Jew repeats the prayer for material prosperity and the promise of ultimate glory: "Thou shalt lend unto many nations but thou shalt not borrow; and thou shalt rule over many nations but they shall not rule over thee." "Our Father, our King," he prays at the New Year, "avenge before our eyes the blood of Thy servants that has been spilt." And at the Passover Seder Service he still repeats the Psalmist's appeal to God to pour out His wrath on the heathen who have consumed Jacob and laid waste his dwelling. "Pursue them in anger and destroy them from under the heavens of the Lord!"

II

Much might, of course, be adduced to mitigate the seeming ferocity or egotism of these passages. It would be indeed strange if Prussia, which Napoleon wittily described as "hatched from a cannon-ball," should be found really resembling Judæa, whose national greeting was "Peace"; whose prophet Ezekiel proclaimed in words of flame and thunder God's judgment upon the great military empires of antiquity; whose mediæval poet Kalir has left in our New Year liturgy what might be almost a contemporary picture of a brazen autocracy "that planned in secret, performed in daring." And, as a matter of fact, some of these passages are torn from their context. The pictures of Messianic prosperity, for example, are invariably set in an ethical framework: the all-dominant Israel is also to be all-righteous. The blood that is to be avenged is the blood of martyrs "who went through fire and water for the sanctification of Thy name."

But let us take these passages at their nakedest. Let us ignore—as completely as Jesus did—that the legal penalty of "eye for eye" had been commuted into a money penalty by the great majority of early Pharisaic lawyers. Is not that very maxim to-day the clamoured policy of Christian multitudes? "Destroy them from under the heavens of the Lord!" When this is the imprecation of a Vehaeren or a Maeterlinck over Belgium and not of a mediæval Jew over the desolated home of Jacob, is it not felt as a righteous cry of the heart? Nay, only the other Sunday an Englishwoman in a country drawing-room assured me she would like to kill every German—man or woman—with her own hand!

And here we see the absurdity of judging the Bible outside its historic conditions, or by standards not comparative. Said James Hinton, "The Bible needs interpreting by Nature even as Nature by it." And it is by this canon that we must interpret the concept of a Chosen People, and so much else in our Scriptures. It is Life alone that can give us the clue to the Bible. This is the only "Guide to the Perplexed," and Maimonides but made confusion worse confounded when by allegations of allegory and other devices of the apologist he laboured to reconcile the Bible with Aristotle. Equally futile was the effort of Manasseh ben Israel to reconcile it with itself. The *Baraitha* of Rabbi Ishmael that when two texts are discrepant a third text must be found to reconcile them is but a temptation to that distorted dialectic known as *Pilpul*. The only true "Conciliador" is history, the only real reconciler human nature.

An allegorizing rationalism like Rambam's leads nowhere—or rather everywhere. The same method that softened the Oriental amorousness of "The Song of Solomon" into an allegory of God's love for Israel became, in the hands of Christianity, an allegory of Christ's love for His Church. But if Reason cannot always—as Bachya imagined—*confirm* tradition, it can explain it historically. It can disentangle the lower strands from the higher in that motley collection of national literature which, extending over many generations of authorship, streaked with strayed fragments of Aramaic, varying from the idyll of Ruth to the apocalyptic dreams of Daniel, and deprived by Job and Ecclesiastes of even a rambling epical unity, is naturally obnoxious to criticism when put forward as one uniform Book, still more when put forward as uniformly divine. For my part I am more lost in wonder over the people that produced and preserved and the Synagogue that selected and canonized so marvellous a literature, than dismayed because occasionally amid the organ-music of its Miltons and Wordsworths there is heard the primeval saga-note of heroic savagery.

III

As Joseph Jacobs reminded us in his "Biblical Archæology" and as Sir James Frazer is just illustrating afresh, the whole of Hebrew ritual is permeated by savage survivals, a fact recognized by Maimonides himself when he declared that Moses adapted idolatrous practices to a purer worship. Israel was environed by barbarous practices and gradually rose beyond them. And it was the same with concepts as with practices. Judaism, which added to the Bible the fruits of centuries of spiritual evolution in the shape of the Talmud, has passed utterly beyond the more primitive stages of the Old Testament, even as it has replaced polygamy by monogamy. That Song of Hate at the Red Sea was wiped out, for example, by the oft-quoted Midrash in which God rebukes the angels who wished to join in the song. "How can ye sing when My creatures are perishing?" The very miracles of the Old Testament were side-tracked by the Rabbinic exposition that they were merely special creations antecedent to that unchangeable system of nature which went its course, however fools suffered. Our daily bread, said the sages, is as miraculous as the division of the Red Sea. And the dry retort of the soberest of Pharisaic Rabbis, when a voice from heaven interfered with the voting on a legal point, *en mashgîchin be-bathkol*—"We cannot have regard to the Bath Kol, the Torah is for earth, not heaven"—was a sign that, for one school of thought at least, reason and the democratic principle were not to be browbeaten, and that the era of miracles in Judaism was over. The very incoherence of the Talmud, its confusion of voices, is an index of free thinking. Post-biblical Israel has had a veritable galaxy of thinkers and saints, from Maimonides its Aquinas to Crescas its Duns Scotus, from Mendelssohn its Erasmus to the Baal-Shem its St. Francis. But it has been at once the weakness and the strength of orthodox Judaism never to have made a breach with its past; possibly out of too great a reverence for history, possibly out of over-consideration for the masses, whose mentality would in any case have transformed the new back again to the old. Thus it has carried its whole lumber piously forward, even as the human body is, according to evolutionists, "a veritable museum of relics," or as whales have vestiges of hind legs with now immovable, muscles. Already in the Persian period Judaism had begun to evolve "the service of the Synagogue," but it did not shed the animal sacrifices, and even when these were abruptly ended by the destruction of the Temple, and Jochanan ben Zaccai must needs substitute prayer and charity, Judaism still preserved through the ages the nominal hope of their restoration. So that even were the Jehovah of the Old Testament the fee-fi-fo-fum ogre of popular imagination, that tyrant of the heavens whose unfairness in choosing Israel was only equalled by its bad taste, it would not follow that Judaism had not silently replaced him by a nobler Deity centuries ago. The truth is, however, that it is precisely in the Old Testament that is reached the highest ethical note ever yet sounded, not only by Judaism but by man, and that this mass of literature is so saturated with the conception of a people chosen not for its own but for universal salvation, that the more material prophecies—evoked moreover in the bitterness of exile, as Belgian poets are now moved to foretell restoration and glory—are practically swamped. At the worst, we may say there are two conflicting currents of thought, as there are in the bosom of every nation, one primarily self- regarding, and the other setting towards the larger life of humanity. It may help us to understand the paradox of the junction of Israel's glory with God's, if we remember that the most inspired of mortals, those whose life is consecrated to an art, a social reform, a political redemption, are rarely able to separate the success of their mission from their own individual success or at least individual importance. Even Jesus looked forward to his twelve legions of angels and his seat at the right hand of Power. But in no other nation known to history has the balance of motives been cast so overwhelmingly on the side of idealism. An episode related by Josephus touching Pontius Pilate serves to illuminate the more famous episode in which he figures. When he brought the Roman ensigns with Cæsar's effigies to Jerusalem, the Jews so wearied him with their petitions to remove this defiling deification that at last he surrounded the petitioners with soldiers and menaced them with immediate death unless they ceased to pester and went home. "But they threw themselves upon the ground and laid their necks bare and said they would take their deaths very willingly rather than the wisdom of their laws should be transgressed." And Pilate, touched, removed the effigies. Such a story explains at once how the Jews could produce Jesus and why they could not worship him.

"God's witnesses," "a light of the nations," "a suffering servant," "a kingdom of priests"—the old Testament metaphors for Israel's mission are as numerous as they are noble. And the lyrics in which they occur are unparalleled in literature for their fusion of ethical passion with poetical beauty. Take, for example, the forty-second chapter of Isaiah. (I quote as in gratitude bound the accurate Jewish version of the Bible we owe to America.)

> Behold My servant whom I uphold;
> Mine elect in whom My soul delighteth;
> I have put My spirit upon him,
> He shall make the right to go forth to the
>   nations:
> He shall not fail or be crushed
> Till he have set the right on the earth,
> And the isles shall wait for his teaching.
> Thus saith God the LORD,
> He that created the heavens, and stretched
>   them forth,
> He that spread forth the earth and that which
>   cometh out of it,
> He that giveth bread unto the people upon it,
> And spirit to them that walk therein:
> I the LORD have called thee in righteousness,
> And have taken hold of thy hand,
> And kept thee, and set thee for a covenant of
>   the people,
> For a light of the nations;
>
> To open the blind eyes,
> To bring out the prisoners from the dungeon,
> And them that sit in darkness out of the

12

prison-house.

Never was ideal less tribal: it is still the dynamic impulse of all civilization. "Let justice well up as waters and righteousness as a mighty stream." "Nation shall not lift sword against nation, neither shall there be war any more."

Nor does this mission march always with the pageantry of external triumph. "Despised and forsaken of men," Isaiah paints Israel. "Yet he bore the sin of many. And made intercession for the transgressors … with his stripes we were healed."

Happily all that is best in Christendom recognizes, with Kuenen or Matthew Arnold, the grandeur of the Old Testament ideal. But that this ideal penetrated equally to our everyday liturgy is less understood of the world. "Blessed art Thou, O Lord our God, who hast chosen Israel from all peoples and given him the Law." Here is no choice of a favourite but of a servant, and when it is added that "from Zion shall the Law go forth" it is obvious what that servant's task is to be. "What everlasting love hast Thou loved the house of Israel," says the Evening Prayer. But in what does this love consist? Is it that we have been pampered, cosseted? The contrary. "A Law, and commandments, statutes and judgments hast Thou taught us." Before these were thundered from Sinai, the historian of the Exodus records, Israel was explicitly informed that only by obedience to them could he enjoy peculiar favour. "Now therefore, if ye will hearken unto My voice indeed, and keep My covenant, then ye shall be Mine own treasure from among all peoples; for all the earth is Mine; and ye shall be unto Me a kingdom of priests, and a holy nation." A chosen people is really a choosing people. Not idly does Talmudical legend assert that the Law was offered first to all other nations and only Israel accepted the yoke.

How far the discipline of the Law actually produced the Chosen People postulated in its conferment is a subtle question for pragmatists. Mr. Lucien Wolf once urged that "the yoke of the Torah" had fashioned a racial aristocracy possessing marked biological advantages over average humanity, as well as sociological superiorities of temperance and family life. And indeed the statistics of Jewish vitality and brain-power, and even of artistic faculty, are amazing enough to invite investigation from all eugenists, biologists, and statesmen. But whether this general superiority—a superiority not inconsistent with grave failings and drawbacks—is due to the rigorous selection of a tragic history, or whether it is, as Anatole Leroy-Beaulieu maintains, the heritage of a civilization older by thousands of years than that of Europe; whether the Torah made the greatness of the people, or the people
—precisely because of its greatness—made the Torah; whether we have a case of natural election or artificial election to study, it is not in any self-

sufficient superiority or aim thereat that the essence of Judaism lies, but in an apostolic altruism. The old Hebrew writers indeed—when one considers the impress the Bible was destined to make on the faith, art, and imagination of the world—might well be credited with the intuition of genius in attributing to their people a quality of election. And the Jews of to-day in attributing to themselves that quality would have the ground not only of intuition but of history. Nevertheless that election is, even by Jewish orthodoxy, conceived as designed solely for world-service, for that spiritual mission for which Israel when fashioned was exiled and scattered like wind-borne seeds, and of the consummation of which his ultimate repatriation and glory will be but the symbol. It is with *Alenu* that every service ends—the prayer for the coming of the Kingdom of God, "when Thou wilt remove the abominations from the earth, and the idols will be utterly cut off, when the world will be perfected under the Kingdom of the Almighty and all the children of flesh will call upon Thy name, when Thou wilt turn unto Thyself all the wicked of the earth.... In that day the Lord shall be One and His name One." Israel disappears altogether in this diurnal aspiration.

IV

Israel disappears, too, in whole books of the Old Testament. What has the problem of Job, the wisdom of Proverbs, or the pessimism of Ecclesiastes to do with the Jew specifically? The Psalter would scarcely have had so universal an appeal had it been essentially rooted in a race.

In the magnificent cosmic poem of Psalm civ—half Whitman, half St. Francis—not only his fellow-man but all creation comes under the benediction of the Hebrew poet's mood. "The high hills are for the wild goats; the rocks are a refuge for the conies.... The young lions roar after their prey, and seek their food from God ... man goeth forth unto his work, and to his labour until the evening." Even in a more primitive Hebrew poet the same cosmic universalism reveals itself. To the bard of Genesis the rainbow betokens not merely a covenant between God and man but a "covenant between God and every living creature of all flesh that is upon the earth."

That the myth of the tribalism of the Jewish God should persist in face of such passages can only be explained by the fact that He shares in the unpopularity of His people. Mr. Wells, for example, in his finely felt but intellectually incoherent book, "God the Invisible King," dismisses Him as a malignant and partisan Deity, jealous and pettily stringent. At most one is entitled to say with Mr. Israel Abrahams in his profound little book on "Judaism" that "God, in the early literature a tribal, non-moral Deity, was in the later literature a righteous ruler, who, with Amos and Hosea, loved and demanded righteousness in man," and that there was an expansion from a national to a universal Ruler. But if "by early literature" anybody understand simply Genesis, if he imagines that the evolutionary movement in Judaism proceeds regularly from Abraham to Isaiah, he is grossly in error. No doubt all early gods are tribal, all early religions connected with the hearth and ancestor worship, but the God of Isaiah is already in Genesis, and the tribal God has to be exhumed from practically all parts of the Bible. But even in the crudities of Genesis or Judges that have escaped editorship I cannot find Mr. Wells's "malignant" Deity—*He* is really "the invisible King." The very first time Jehovah appears in His tribal aspect (Genesis xii.) His promise to bless Abraham ends with the assurance—and it almost invariably accompanies all the repetitions of the promise—"And in thee shall all the families of the earth be blessed." Nay, as I pointed out in my essay on "The Gods of Germany," the very first words of the Bible, "In the beginning God created the heaven and the earth," strike a magnificent note of universalism, which is sustained in the derivation of all humanity from Adam, and again from Noah, with one original language. Nor is this a modern gloss, for the Talmud already deduces the interpretation. Racine's "Esther" in the noble lines lauded by Voltaire might be almost rebuking Mr. Wells:—

> Ce Dieu, maître absolu de la terre et des cieux,
> N'est point tel que l'erreur le figure à vos
>   yeux:
> L'Eternel est son nom, le monde est son
>   ouvrage;
> Il entend les soupirs de l'humble qu'on
>   outrage,
> Juge tous les mortels avec d'égales lois,
> Et du haut de son trône interroge les rois.

—there is the true Hebrew note, the note denounced of Nietzsche.

Is this notorious "tribal God" the God of the Mesopotamian sheikh whose seed was so invidiously chosen? Well, but of this God Abraham asks—in what I must continue to call the epochal sentence in the Bible—"Shall not the Judge of all the earth do right?" Abraham, in fact, bids God down as in some divine Dutch auction—Sodom is not to be destroyed if it holds fifty, forty- five, forty, thirty, twenty, nay ten righteous men. Compare this ethical development of the ancestor of Judaism with that of Pope Gregory XIII, in the sixteenth century, some thirty-one centuries later: *Civitas ista potest esse destrui quando in ea plures sunt hæretici* ("A city may be destroyed when it harbours a number of heretics"). And this claim of man to criticize God Jehovah freely concedes. Thus the God of Abraham is no God of a tribe, but, like the God of the Rabbi who protested against the Bath-Kol, the God of Reason and Love. As clearly as for the nineteenth-century Martineau, "the seat of authority in Religion" has passed to the human conscience. God Himself appeals to it in that inversion of the Sodom story, the story of Jonah, whose teaching is far greater and more wonderful than its fish. And this Abrahamic tradition of free thought is continued by Moses, who boldly comes between Jehovah and the people He designs to destroy. "Wherefore should the Egyptians speak, saying, For evil did He bring them forth to slay them in the mountains…? Turn from Thy fierce wrath and repent of this evil against Thy people." Moses goes on to remind Him of the covenant, "And the Lord repented of the evil which He said He would do unto His people." In the same chapter, the people having made a golden calf, Moses offers his life for their sin; the Old Testament here, as in so many places, anticipating the so-called New, but rejecting the notion of vicarious atonement so drastically that the attempt of dogmatic Christianity to base itself on the Old Testament can only be described as text-blind. And the great answer of Jehovah to Moses's questioning—"I AM THAT I AM"— yields already the profound metaphysical Deity of Maimonides, that "invisible King" whom the anonymous New Year liturgist celebrates as:

> Highest divinity,
> Dynast of endlessness,
> Timeless resplendency,
> Worshipped eternally,
> Lord of Infinity!

And the fact that Moses himself was married to an Egyptian woman and that "a mixed multitude" went up with the Jews out of Egypt shows that the narrow tribalism of Ezra and Nehemiah, with the regrettable rejection of the Samaritans, was but a temporary political necessity; while the subsequent admission into the canon of the book of "Ruth," with its moral of the descent of the Messiah himself from a Moabite woman, is an index that universalism was still unconquered. We have, in fact, the recurring clash of centripetal and centrifugal forces, and what assured the persistence and assures the ultimate

16

triumph of the latter is that the race being one with the religion could not resist that religion's universal implications. If there were only a single God, and He a God of justice and the world, how could He be confined to Israel? The Mission could not but come. The true God, urges Mr. Wells, has no scorn or hatred for those who seek Him through idols. That is exactly what Ibn Gabirol said in 1050. But those blind seekers needed guiding. Religion, in fact, not race, has always been the governing principle in Jewish history. "I do not know the origin of the term Jew," says Dion Cassius, born in the second century. "The name is used, however, to designate all who observe the customs of this people, even though they be of different race." Where indeed lay the privilege of the Chosen People when the Talmud defined a non- idolater as a Jew, and ranked a Gentile learned in the Torah as greater than the High Priest? Such learned proselytes arose in Aquila and Theodotion each of whom made a Greek version of the Bible; while the orthodox Jew hardly regards his Hebrew text as complete unless accompanied by the Aramaic version popularly ascribed to the proselyte Onkelos. The disagreeable references to proselytes in Rabbinic literature, the difficulties thrown in their way, and the grotesque conception of their status towards their former families, cannot counterbalance the fact, established by Radin in his learned work, "The Jews Among the Greeks and Romans," that there was a carefully planned effort of propaganda. Does not indeed Jesus tell the Pharisees: "Ye compass sea and land to make one proselyte"? Do not Juvenal and Horace complain of this Judaising? Were not the Idumeans proselytised almost by force? "The Sabbath and the Jewish fasts," says Lecky, doubtless following Josephus, "became familiar facts in all the great cities." And Josephus himself in that answer to Apion, which Judaism has strangely failed to rank as one of its greatest documents, declares in noble language: "There ought to be but one Temple for one God ... and this Temple common to all men, because He is the common God of all men."

It would be a very tough tribal God that could survive worshippers of this temper. An ancient Midrash taught that in the Temple there were seventy sacrifices offered for the seventy nations. For the mediæval and rationalist Maimonides the election of Israel scarcely exists—even the Messiah is only to be a righteous Conqueror, whose success will be the test of his genuineness. And Spinoza—though he, of course, is outside the development of the Synagogue proper—refused to see in the Jew any superiority save of the sociological system for ensuring his eternity. The comparatively modern Chassidism, anticipating Mazzini, teaches that every nation and language has a special channel through which it receives God's gifts. Of contemporary Reform Judaism, the motto "Have we not one father, hath not one God created us?" was formally adopted as the motto of the Congress of Religions at Washington. "The forces of democracy *are* Israel," cries the American Jew, David Lubin, in an ultra-modern adaptation of the Talmudic scale of values. There is, in fact, through our post-biblical literature almost a note of apology for the assumption of the Divine mission: perhaps it is as much the offspring of worldly prudence as of spiritual progress. The Talmud observed that the Law was only given to Israel because he was so peculiarly fierce he needed curbing. Abraham Ibn Daud at the beginning of the twelfth century urged that God had to reveal Himself to some nation to show that He did not hold Himself aloof from the universe, leaving its rule to the stars: it is the very argument as to the need for Christ employed by Mr. Balfour in his "Foundations of Belief." Crescas, in the fourteenth century, declared—like an earlier Buckle—that the excellence of the Jew sprang merely from the excellence of Palestine. Mr. Abelson, in his recent valuable book on Jewish mysticism, alleges that when Rabbi Akiba called the Jews "Sons of God" he meant only that all other nations were idolaters. But in reality Akiba meant what he said—what indeed had been said throughout the Bible from Deuteronomy downwards. In the words of Hosea:

> When Israel was a child, then I loved him,
> And out of Egypt I called My son.

No evidence of the universalism of Israel's mission can away with the fact that it was still *his* mission, the mission of a Chosen People. And this conviction, permeating and penetrating his whole literature and broidering itself with an Oriental exuberance of legendary fantasy, poetic or puerile, takes on in places an intimacy, sometimes touching in its tender mysticism, sometimes almost grotesque in its crude reminder to God that after all His own glory and reputation are bound up with His people's, and that He must not go too far in His chastisements lest the heathen mock. Reversed, this apprehension produced the concept of the *Chillul Hashem*, "the profanation of the Name." Israel, in his turn, was in honour bound not to lower the reputation of the Deity, who had chosen him out. On the contrary, he was to promote the *Kiddush Hashem* "the sanctification of the Name." Thus the doctrine of election made not for arrogance but for a sense of *Noblesse oblige*. As the "Hymn of Glory" recited at New Year says in a more poetic sense: "His glory is on me and mine on Him." "He loves His people," says the hymn, "and inhabits their praises." Indeed, according to Schechter, the ancient Rabbis actually conceived God as existing only through Israel's continuous testimony and ceasing were Israel— *per impossibile*—to disappear. It is a mysticism not without affinity to Mr. Wells's. A Chassidic Rabbi, quoted by Mr. Wassilevsky, teaches in the same spirit that God and Israel, like Father and Son, are each incomplete without the other. In another passage of Hosea—a passage recited at the everyday winding of phylacteries—the imagery is of

18

wedded lovers. "I will betroth thee unto Me for ever, Yea I will betroth thee unto Me in righteousness and in judgment and in loving-kindness and in mercy."

But it is in the glowing, poetic soul of Jehuda Ha-Levi that this election of Israel, like the passion for Palestine, finds its supreme and uncompromising expression. "Israel," declares the author of the "Cuzari" in a famous dictum, "is among the nations like the heart among the limbs." Do not imagine he referred to the heart as a pump, feeding the veins of the nations—Harvey was still five centuries in the future—he meant the heart as the centre of feeling and the symbol of the spirit. And examining the question why Israel had been thus chosen, he declares plumply that it is as little worthy of consideration as why the animals had not been created men. This is, of course, the only answer. The wind of creation and inspiration bloweth where it listeth. As Tennyson said in a similar connection:

> And if it is so, so it is, you know,
> And if it be so, so be it!

V

But although, as with all other manifestations of genius, Science cannot tell us why the Jewish race was so endowed spiritually, it can show us by parallel cases that there is nothing unique in considering yourself a Chosen People— as indeed the accusation with which we began reminds us. And it can show us that a nation's assignment of a mission to itself is not a sudden growth. "Unlike any other nation," says the learned and saintly leader of Reform Judaism, Dr. Kohler, in his article on "Chosen People" in the *Jewish Encyclopædia*, "the Jewish people began their career conscious of their life- purpose and world-duty as the priests and teachers of a universal religious truth." This is indeed a strange statement, and only on the theory that its author was expounding the biblical standpoint, and not his own, can it be reconciled with his general doctrine of progress and evolution in Hebrew thought. It would seem to accept the Sinaitic Covenant as a literal episode, and even to synchronise the Mission with it. But an investigation of the history of other Chosen Peoples will, I fear, dissipate any notion that the Sinaitic Covenant was other than a symbolic summary of the national genius for religion, a sublime legend retrospectively created. And the mission to other nations must have been evolved still later. "The conception or feeling of a mission grew up and was developed by slow degrees," says Mr. Montefiore, and this sounds much nearer the truth. For, as I said, history is the sole clue to the Bible—history, which according to Bacon, is "philosophy teaching by example." And the more modern the history is, and the nearer in time, the better we can understand it. We have before our very eyes the moving spectacle of the newest of nations setting herself through a President-Prophet the noblest mission ever formulated outside the Bible. Through another great prophet—sprung like Amos from the people—through Abraham Lincoln, America had already swept away slavery. I do not know exactly when she began to call herself "God's own country," but her National Anthem, "My Country, 'tis of thee," dating from 1832, fixes the date when America, soon after the second war with England, which ended in 1814, consciously felt herself as a Holy Land; far as visitors like Dickens felt her from the perfection implied in her soaring Spread-Eagle rhetoric. The Pilgrim Fathers went to America merely for their own freedom of religious worship: they were actually intolerant to others. From a sectarian patriotism developed what I have called "The Melting Pot," with its high universal mission, first at home and now over the world at large.

The stages of growth are still more clearly marked in English history. That national self-consciousness which to-day gives itself the mission of defending the liberties of mankind, and which stands in the breach undaunted and indomitable, began with that mere insular patriotism which finds such moving expression in the pæan of Shakespeare:

> This happy breed of men, this little world,
> This precious stone set in the silver sea,
>
> .   .   .   .   .   .
>
> This blessed plot, this earth, this realm, this
> England,
>
> .   .   .   .   .   .
>
> This land of such dear souls, this dear, dear
> land.

This sense of itself had been born only in the thirteenth century, and at first the growing consciousness of national power, though it soon developed an assurance of special protection—"the favour of the love of Heaven," wrote Milton in his "Areopagitica," "we have great argument to think in a peculiar manner propitious and propending towards us"—was tempered by that humility still to be seen in the liturgy of its Church, which ascribes its victories not to the might of the English arm, but to the favour of God. But one hundred and twenty-five years after Shakespeare, the land which the Elizabethan translators of the Bible called "Our Sion," and whose mission, according to Milton, had been to sound forth "the first tidings and trumpet of reformation to all Europe," had sunk to the swaggering militarism that found expression in "Rule, Britannia."

> When Britain first at Heaven's command
> > Arose from out the azure main,
> This was the charter of the land,
> > And guardian angels sung this strain:
> > > Rule, Britannia, rule the waves;
> > > Britons never will be slaves.
> The nations not so blest as thee
>
> > Must in their turn to tyrants fall;
> While thou shalt flourish, great and free,
> > The dread and envy of them all.
>
> To thee belongs the rural reign,
> > Thy cities shall with commerce shine:
> All thine shall be the subject main,
> > And every shore it circles, thine.

It is the true expression of its period—a period which Sir John Seeley in his "Expansion of England" characterizes as the period of the struggle with France for the possession of India and the New World: there were no less than seven wars with France, for France had replaced Spain in that great competition of the five western maritime States of Europe for Transatlantic trade and colonies, in which Seeley sums up the bulk of two centuries of European history. Well may Mr. Chesterton point to the sinking of the Armada as the date when an Old Testament sense of being "answered in stormy oracles of air and sea" lowered Englishmen into a Chosen People. Shakespeare saw the sea serving England in the modest office of a moat: it was now to be the high-road of Empire. The Armada was shattered in 1588. In 1600 the East India Company is formed to trade all over the world. In 1606 is founded the British colony of Virginia and in 1620 New England. It helps us to understand the dual and conflicting energies stimulated in the atmosphere of celestial protection, if we recall that it was in 1604 that was initiated the great Elizabethan translation of the Bible.

In Cromwell, that typical Englishman, these two strands of impulse are seen united. Ever conceiving himself the servant of God, he seized Jamaica in a time of profound peace and in defiance of treaty. Was not Catholic Spain the enemy of God? *Delenda est Carthago* is his feeling towards the rival Holland. Miracles attend his battle. "The Lord by his Providence put a cloud over the

Moon, thereby giving us the opportunity to draw off those horse." Yet this elect of God ruthlessly massacres surrendered Irish garrisons. "Sir," he writes with almost childish naïveté, "God hath taken away your eldest son by a cannon shot." We do not need Carlyle's warning that he was not a hypocrite. Does not Marvell, lamenting his death, record in words curiously like Bismarck's that his deceased hero

> The soldier taught that inward mail to wear
> And fearing God, how they should nothing
> fear?

The fact is that great and masterful souls identify themselves with the universe. And so do great and masterful nations. It is a dangerous tendency.

At the death of Queen Anne England stood at the top of the nations. But it was a greatness tainted by the slave-trade abroad, and poverty, ignorance, and gin-drinking at home. We recapture the atmosphere of "Rule, Britannia" when we recall that Thomson wrote it to the peals of the joy-bells and the flare of the bonfires by which the mob celebrated its forcing Walpole into a war to safeguard British trade in the Spanish main. Seeley claims, indeed, that the growth of the Empire was always sub-conscious or semi-conscious at its best. This is not wholly true, for in "The Masque of Alfred" in which "Rule, Britannia" is enshrined, Thomson displays as keen and exact a sense of the lines of England's destiny as Seeley acquired by painful historic excogitation. For after a vision which irresistibly recalls the grosser Hebrew prophecies:

> I see thy commerce, Britain, grasp the world:
> All nations serve thee; every foreign flood,
> Subjected, pays its tribute to the Thames,

he points to the virgin shores "beyond the vast Atlantic surge" and cries:

> This new world,
> Shook to its centre, trembles at her name:
> And there her sons, with aim exalted, sow
>
> The seeds of rising empire, arts, and arms.
>
> Britons, proceed, the subject deep command,
> Awe with your navies every hostile land.
> Vain are their threats, their armies all are vain:
> They rule the balanced world who rule the
> main.

But you have only to remember that Seeley's famous book was written expressly to persuade the England of 1883 *not* to give up India and the

22

Colonies, to see how little "Rule, Britannia" expressed the truer soul of Britain. The purification of England which the Methodist movement began and which manifested itself, among other things, in sweeping away the slave- trade, necessitated a less crude formula for the still invincible instinct of expansion, and in Kipling a prophet arose, of a genius akin to that of the Old Testament, to spiritualize the doctrine of the Chosen People. The mission which in Thomson is purely self-centred becomes in Kipling almost as universal as the visions of the Hebrew bards.

> The Lord our God Most High,
> He hath made the deep as dry,
> He hath smote for us a pathway to the ends of
> > all the earth.

But it is only as the instrument of His purpose, and that purpose is characteristically practical.

> Keep ye the Law—be swift in all obedience;
> Clear the land of evil, drive the road and
> > bridge the ford,
> > > Make ye sure to each his own,
> > > That he reap where he hath sown;
> By the peace among our peoples let men know
> > we serve the Lord.

And it is a true picture of British activities. Even thus has England on the whole ruled the territories into which adventure or economic motives drew her. The very Ambassador from Germany, Prince Lichnowsky, agrees with Rhodes that the salvation of mankind lies in British imperialism. But note how the less spiritual factors are ignored, how the prophet presents his people as a nation of pioneer martyrs, how the mission, finally become conscious of itself, gilds with backward rays the whole path of national advance, as the trail of light from the stern of a vessel gives the illusion that it has come by a shining road. Missions are not discovered till they are already in action. Not unlike those archers of whom the Talmud wittily says, they first shoot the arrow and then fix the target, nations ascribe to themselves purposes of which they were originally unconscious. First comes the tingling consciousness of achievement and power, then a glamour of retrospective legend to explain and justify it. Thus it is that that great struggle for sea-power to which Spain, Portugal, Holland, England, and France all contributed maritime genius and boundless courage, becomes transformed under the half-accidental success of one nation into an almost religious epic of a destined wave-ruler. There could not be a finer British spirit than Mr. Chesterton's fallen friend, the poet Vernède, yet even he writes:—

God grant to us the old Armada weather.

Thomson was not poet enough—nor the eighteenth century naïve enough—to create a legend in sober earnest. But the fact that he throws "Rule, Britannia" eight centuries back to the time of Alfred the Great, before whom this glorious pageant of his country's future is prophetically unrolled, serves to illustrate the retrospective habit of national missions.

The history of England is brief, and the mission evolved in her seven centuries has not yet finally shaped itself, is indeed now shaping itself afresh in the furnace of war. Her poets have not always troubled with the soul of her. They have often, as Courthope complained of Keats, turned away from her destinies to

> Magic casements opening on the foam
> Of faëry lands in perilous seas forlorn.

But Israel had abundant time to perfect her conception of herself. From Moses to Ezra was over a thousand years, and the roots of the race are placed still earlier. Can we doubt it was by a process analogous to that we see at work in England, that Israel evolved into a People chosen for world-service? The Covenant of Israel was inscribed slowly in the Jewish heart: it had no more existence elsewhere than the New Covenant which Jeremiah announced the Lord would write there, no more objective reality than the Charter which Britain received when "first at Heaven's command" she "rose from out the azure main," or than that *Contrat Social* by which Rousseau expressed the rights of the individual in society. But to say this is not to make the mission false. Ibsen might label these vitalizing impulses "Life-illusions," but the criteria of objective truth do not apply to volitional verities. National missions become false only when nations are false to them. Nor does the gradualness of their evolution rob them of their mystery. *Hamlet* is not less inspired because Shakespeare began as a writer of pothooks and hangers.

If it is suggested that to explain the Bible by men and nations under its spell is to reason in a circle, the answer is that the biblical vocabulary merely provides a medium of expression for a universal tendency. Claudian, addressing the Emperor Theodosius, wrote:—

> O nimium dilecte deo, cui militat æther.

The Egyptian god Ammon, in the great battle epic of Rameses II, assured the monarch:—

> Lo, I am with thee, my son; fear not, Ramessu
>   Miammon!
> Ra, thy father, is with thee, his hand shall
>   uphold thee in danger,
> More am I worth unto thee than thousands and
>   thousands of soldiers.

The preamble to the modern Japanese Constitution declares it to be "in pursuance of a great policy co-extensive with the Heavens and the Earth."

25

VI

Returning now finally to our starting-point, the proposition that "Germanism is Judaism," we are able to see its full grotesqueness. If Germanism resembles Judaism, it is as a monkey resembles a man. Where it does suggest Judaism is in the sense it gives the meanest of its citizens that they form part of a great historic organism, which moves to great purposes: a sense which the poorer Englishman has unfortunately lacked, and which is only now awakening in the common British breast. But even here the affinities of Germany are rather with Japan than with Judæa. For in Japan, too, beneath all the romance of Bushido and the Samurai, lies the asphyxiation of the individual and his sacrifice to the State. It is the resurrection of those ancient Pagan Constitutions for which individuality scarcely existed, which could expose infants or kill off old men because the State was the supreme ethical end; it is the revival on a greater scale of the mediæval city commune, which sucked its vigorous life from the veins of its citizens. Even so Prussia, by welding its subservient citizens into one gigantic machine of aggression, has given a new reading to the Gospel: "Blessed are the meek, for they shall inherit the earth."

Nietzsche, who, though he strove to upset the old Hebrew values, saw clearly through the real Prussian peril, defined such a State as that "in which the slow suicide of all is called Life," and "a welcome service unto all preachers of death"—a cold, ill-smelling, monstrous idol. Nor is this the only affinity between Prussia and Japan. "We are," boasts a Japanese writer, "a people of the present and the Tangible, of the Broad Daylight and the Plainly Visible."

But Germany was not always thus. "High deeds, O Germans, are to come from you," wrote Wordsworth in his "Sonnets dedicated to Liberty." And it throws light upon the nature of Missions to recall that when she lay at the feet of Napoleon after Jena, the mission proclaimed for her by Fichte was one of peace and righteousness—to penetrate the life of humanity by her religion— and he denounced the dreams of universal monarchy which would destroy national individuality. Calling on his people as "the consecrated and inspired ones of a Divine world-plan," "To you," he says, "out of all other modern nations the germs of human perfection are especially committed. It is yours to found an empire of mind and reason—to destroy the dominion of rude physical power as the ruler of the world." And throwing this mission backwards, he sees in what the outer world calls the invasion of the Roman Empire by the Goths and Huns the proof that the Germans have always stemmed the tide of tyrant domination. But Fichte belonged to the generation of Kant and Beethoven. Hegel, coming a little later, though as non-nationalist as Goethe, and a welcomer of the Napoleonic invasion, yet prophesied that if the Germans were once forced to cast off their inertia, they, "by preserving in their contact with outward things the intensity of their inner life, will perchance surpass their teachers": and in curiously prophetic language he called for a hero "to realize by blood and iron the political regeneration of Germany."

If Treitschke, too, believed in force, he had a high moral ideal for his nation. The other nations are feeble and decadent. Germany is to hold the sceptre of the nations, so as to ensure the peace of the world. It is only in Bernhardi that we find war in itself glorified as the stimulus of nations. Even this ideal has a perverted nobility; as Pol Arcas, a modern Greek writer, says: "If the devil knew he had horns the cherubim would offer him their place." And though it was only in the swelled head of the conqueror that the brutal philosophy of the Will-to-Power germinated, it was not so much the "blood and iron" of Junkerdom that perverted Prussia—Junkerdom still lives simply —as the gross industrial prosperity that followed on the victory of 1870. A modern German author describes his countrymen—it is true he has turned Mohammedan, probably out of disgust—as tragically degenerated and turned into a gold-greedy, pleasure-seeking, title-hungry pack. This industrial transformation of the nobler soul of Germany is by Verhaeren—attacking Judaism from another angle—ascribed to its Jews, so it is comforting to remember that when England started the East India Company there was scarcely a Jew in England. No, Germany is clearly where England was in the seventeenth century, and in Prussia England meets her past face to face. Her past, but infinitely more conscious and consequent than her "Rule, Britannia" period, with a ruthless logic that does not shrink from any conclusions. While England's right hand hardly knew what her left was doing, Germany's right hand is drawing up a philosophic justification of her sinister activities. There is in Henry James's posthumous novel—"The Sense of the Past"—a young man who gets locked up in the Past and cannot get back to his own era. This is the fate that now menaces civilization. Nor is the civilization that followed the struggle for America by the scramble for Africa entirely blameless. Germany, federated too late for the first mêlée and smarting under centuries of humiliation—did not Louis XIV insolently seize Strassburg?—is avenging on our century the sins of the seventeenth.

So far from Germanism being synonymous with Judaism, its analogies are to be sought within the five maritime countries which preceded Germany, albeit less efficiently, in the path of militarism. It is the same alliance as prevailed everywhere between the traders and the armies and navies, and the Kaiser's crime consists mainly in turning back the movement of the world which through the Hague Conferences was approaching brotherhood, or at least a mitigation of the horrors of war. His blasphemies are no less archaic. He repeats Oliver Cromwell, but with less simplicity, while his artistic aspiration complicates the Puritan with the Cavalier. "From childhood," he is quoted as saying, "I have been under the influence of five men—Alexander, Julius Cæsar, Theodoric II, Frederick the Great, and Napoleon." No great man moulds himself thus like others. It is but a theatrical greatness. But anyhow none of these names are Jewish, and not thus were "the Kings of Jerusalem" even "six thousand years ago." Our kings had the dull duty of copying out and studying the Torah, and the Rabbis reminded monarchy that the Torah demands forty-eight qualifications, whereas royalty only thirty, and that the crown of a good name is the best of all. Compare the German National Anthem "Heil dir im Siegeskranz" with the noble prayer for the Jewish King in the seventy-second psalm, if you wish to understand the difference between Judaism and Germanism. This King, too, is to conquer his enemies, but he is also to redeem the needy from oppression and violence, "and precious will their blood be in his sight."

———————

VII

If I were asked to sum up in a word the essential difference between Judaism and Germanism, it would be the word "Recessional." While the prophets and historians of Germany monotonously glorify their nation, the Jewish writers as monotonously rebuke theirs. "You only have I known among all the families of the earth," says the message through Amos. "*Therefore* I will visit upon you all your iniquities." The Bible, as I have said before, is an anti-Semitic book. "Israel is the villain, not the hero, of his own story." Alone among epics, it is out for truth, not high heroics. To flout the Pharisees was not reserved for Jesus. "Behold, ye fast for strife and contention," said Isaiah, "and to smite with the fist of wickedness." While some German writers, not content with the great men Germany has so abundantly produced, vaunt that all others, from Jesus to Dante, from Montaigne to Michael Angelo, are of Teuton blood, Jewish literature unflinchingly exposes the flaws even of a Moses and a David. It is this passion for veracity unknown among other peoples—is even Washington's story told without gloss?—that gives false colour to the legend of Israel's ancient savagery. "The title of a nation to its territory," says Seeley, "is generally to be sought in primitive times and would be found, if we could recover it, to rest upon violence and massacre." The dispossession of the Red Indian by America, of the Maori by New Zealand, is almost within living memory. But in national legends this universal process is sophisticated.

> Tu regere imperio populos, Romane,
> memento,

the Æneid told the all-invading Roman, putting of course the contemporary ideal backwards—as all missons are put—and into the prophetic mouth of Jove:—

> Hae tibi erunt artis, pacisque imponere
> morem,
> Parcere subjectis et debelare superbos.

It was for similarly exalted purposes that Israel was to occupy Palestine, yet with what unique denigration the Bible turns upon him: "Not for thy righteousness or for the uprightness of thy heart dost thou go to possess this land; but for the wickedness of these nations the Lord thy God doth drive them out from before thee."

In English literature this note of "Recessional" was sounded long before Kipling. Milton, though he claimed that "God's manner" was to reveal himself "first to His Englishmen," added that they "mark not the methods of His counsel and are unworthy."

"Is India free," wrote Cowper, "or do we grind her still?" "Secure from actual warfare," sang Coleridge, "we have loved to swell the war-whoop." For Wordsworth England was simply the least evil of the nations. And Mr. Chesterton has just written a "History of England" in the very spirit of a Micah flagellating the classes "who loved fields and seized them." But if in Germany a voice of criticism breaks the chorus of self-adoration, it is usually from a Jew like Maximilian Harden, for Jews, as Ambassador Gerard testifies, represent almost the only real culture in Germany. I have been at pains to examine the literature of the German Synagogue, which if Germanism were Judiasm, ought to show a double dose of original sin. But so far from finding any swagger of a Chosen People, whether Jewish or German,

I find in its most popular work—Lazarus's "Soziale Ethik im Judentum"—published as late as November, 1913, by the League of German Jews—a grave indictment of militarism. For the venerable philosopher, while justly explaining the glamour of the army by its subordination of the individual to the communal weal, yet pointed out emphatically that what unites individuals separates nations. "The work of justice shall be peace," he quotes from Isaiah. I am far from supposing that the old Germany of Goethe and Schiller and Lessing is not still latent—indeed, we know that one Professor suggested at a recent Nietzsche anniversary that the Germans should try to rise not to Supermen but to Men, and that another now lies in prison for explaining in his "Biologie des Krieges" that the real objection to war is simply that it compels men to act unlike men. So that, when moreover we remember that the noblest and most practical treatise on "Perpetual Peace" came from that other German professor, Kant, the hope is not altogether *ausgechlossen* that in the internal convulsion that must follow the war, there may be an upheaval of that finer Germanism of which we should be only too proud to say that it *is* Judaism.

VIII

But meantime we are waiting, and the soul "waiteth for the Lord more than watchmen look for the morning, yea, more than watchmen for the morning." Again, as in earlier periods of history, the world lies in darkness, listening to the silence of God—a silence that can be felt.

"Watchmen, what of the night?" Such a blackness fell upon the ancient Jews when Hadrian passed the plough over Mount Zion. But, turning from empty apocalyptic visions, they drew in on themselves and created an inner Jerusalem, which has solaced and safeguarded them ever since. Such a blackness fell on the ancient Christians when the Huns invaded Rome, and the young Christian world, robbed of its millennial hopes, began to wonder if perchance this was not the vengeance of the discarded gods. But drawing in on themselves, they learned from St. Augustine to create an inner "City of God." How shall humanity meet this blackest crisis of all? What new "City of

God" can it build on the tragic wreckage of a thousand years of civilization? Has Israel no contribution to offer here but the old quarrel with Christianity? But that quarrel shrinks into comparative concord beside the common peril from the resurrected gods of paganism, from Thor and Odin and Priapus. And it was always an exaggerated quarrel—half misunderstanding, like most quarrels. Neither St. Augustine nor St. Anselm believed God was other than One. Jesus but applied to himself distributively—as logicians say—those conceptions of divine sonship and suffering service which were already assets of Judaism, and but for the theology of atonement woven by Paul under Greek influences, either of them might have carried Judaism forward on that path of universalism which its essential genius demands, and which even without them it only just missed. Is it not humiliating that Islam, whose Koran expressly recalls its obligation to our prophets, should have beaten them in the work of universalization? Maimonides acknowledged the good work done by Jesus and Mohammed in propagating the Bible. But if the universalism they achieved held faulty elements, is that any reason why the purer truth should shrink from universalization? Has Judaism less future than Buddhism—that religion of negation and monkery—whose sacred classics enjoin the Bhiksu to camp in and contemplate a cemetery? Has it less inspiration and optimism than that apocalyptic vision of the ultimate victory of Good which consoles the disciples of Zoroaster? If there is anything now discredited in its ancient Scriptures, the Synagogue can, as of yore, relegate it to the Apocrypha, even as it can enrich the canon with later expressions of the Hebrew genius. Its one possible rival, Islam, is, as Kuenen maintains, as sterile for the future as Buddhism, too irretrievably narrowed to the Arab mentality. But why, despite his magnificent tribute to Judaism, does this unfettered thinker imagine that the last word is with Christianity? Eucken, too, would call the future Christian, though he rejects the Incarnation and regards the Atonement as injurious to religion, and the doctrine of the Trinity as a stumbling-block rather than a help. Abraham Lincoln being only a plain man, was not able to juggle with himself like a German theologian, and with the simplicity of greatness he confessed: "I have never united myself to any Church, because I have found difficulty in giving my assent, without mental reservation, to the long, complicated statements of the Christian doctrine which characterize their Articles of Belief and Confessions of Faith." "When any church," he added, "will inscribe over its altar, as its sole qualification for membership, … 'Thou shalt love the Lord thy God with all thy heart, and with all thy soul, and with all thy might, and thy neighbour as thyself,' that church will I join with all my heart and with all my soul."

Can one read this and not wonder what Judaism has been about that Lincoln did not even know there *was* such a church? But call the coming religious reconstruction what you will, what do names matter when all humanity is crucified, what does anything matter but to save it from meaningless frictions and massacres? "Would that My people forgot Me and kept My commandments," says the Jerusalem Talmud. Too long has Israel been silent. "Who is blind," says the prophet, "but My servant, or deaf as My messenger?" He is not deaf to-day, he is only dumb. But the voice of Jerusalem must be heard again when the new world-order is shaping. The Chosen People must choose. To be or not to be. "The religion of the Jews is indeed a light," said Coleridge in his "Table Talk," "but it is as the light of the glow-worm which gives no heat and illumines nothing but itself." Why let a sun sink into a glow-worm? And even a glow-worm should turn. It does not even pay—that prudent maxim of the Babylonian Talmud, *Dina dimalchutha dina* ("In Rome do as the Romans"). Despite every effort of Jews as individual citizens the world still tends to see them as Crabbe saw them a century ago in his "Borough":—

> Nor war nor wisdom yields our Jews delight,
>
> They will not study and they dare not fight.

It is because they fight under no banner of their own. But the time has come when they must fight as Jews—fight that "mental fight" from which that greater English poet, Blake, declared he would not cease till he had "built Jerusalem in England's green and pleasant land." To build Jerusalem in every land—even in Palestine—that is the Jewish mission. As Nina Salaman sings —and I am glad to end with the words of a daughter of the lofty-souled scholar in whose honour this lecture is given—

> Wherefore else our age-long life, our
> wandering landless,
> Every land our home for ill or good?
> Ours it was long since to join the hands of
> nations
> Through the link of our own brotherhood.

AFTERWORD

AFTERWORD

Dr. Israel Abrahams, Reader in Talmudic and Rabbinic Literature in the University of Cambridge, in seconding the vote of thanks to the speakers, moved by the President of the Jewish Historical Society (Sir Lionel Abrahams, K.C.B.), said that the Chairman had already paid a tribute to the memory of Arthur Davis. But a twice-told tale was not stale in repetition when the tale was told of such a man. He was a real scholar; not only in the general sense of one who loved great books, but also in the special sense that he possessed the technical knowledge of an expert. His "Hebrew Accents" reveals Arthur Davis in these two aspects. It shows mastery of an intricate subject, a subject not likely to attract the mere dilettante. But it also reveals his interest in the Bible as literature. He appreciated both the music of words and the melody of ideas. When the work appeared, a foreign scholar asked: "Who was his teacher?" The answer was: himself. There is a rather silly proverb that the self-taught man has a fool for his master. Certainly Arthur Davis had no fool for his pupil. And though he had no teacher, he had what is better, a fine capacity for comradeship in studies. "Acquire for thyself a companion," said the ancient Rabbi. There is no friendship equal to that which is made over the common study of books. At the Talmud meetings held at the house of Arthur Davis were founded lifelong intimacies. Unpretentious in their aim, there was in these gatherings a harmony of charm and earnestness; pervading them was the true "joy of service." Above all he loved the liturgy. Here the self-taught man must excel. Homer said:—

> Dear to gods and men is sacred song.
> Self-taught I sing: by Heaven and Heaven
> alone
> The genuine seeds of poesy are sown.

And, as the expression of his inmost self, he gave us the best edition of the Festival Prayers in any language: better than Sachs'—than which praise can go no higher. This Prayer Book is his true memorial, unless there be a truer still. Perhaps his feeling that he might after all have lost something because he had no teacher made him so wonderful a teacher of his own daughters. In their continuance of his work his personality endures. At the end of his book on Accents he quoted, in Hebrew, a sentence from Jeremiah, with a clever play on the double meaning of the word which signifies at once "accent" and "taste." Thinking of his record, and how his beautiful spirit animates those near and dear to him, we may indeed apply to him this same text: "His taste remaineth in him and his fragrance is not changed."